Weekly Reader Children's Book Club presents

GUS WAS A MEXICAN GHOST

BY JANE THAYER
PICTURES BY SEYMOUR FLEISHMAN

WILLIAM MORROW & COMPANY
NEW YORK 1974

Woolley, Catherine.
  Gus was a Mexican ghost.

  SUMMARY: The adventures of Gus the ghost
who takes a trip to Mexico.
  [1. Ghost stories. 2. Mexico—Fiction]
I. Fleishman, Seymour, illus. II. Title.
PZ7.W882Gv   [E]   73-14587
ISBN 0-688-20104-0
ISBN 0-688-30104-5 (lib. bdg.)

Weekly Reader Children's Book Club Edition

Gus the ghost
     lived in the Historical Museum
with Cora the cat, Mouse the mouse,
Baby Ghost, and Mr. Frizzle.
He was happy there,
even though Mr. Frizzle
had a terrible temper and shouted.
Shouting made Frizzle feel better,
so when he didn't shout
at least once a day,
Gus wondered what was wrong.
In summer many people came to see
the spinning wheel, old cradle,
grandfather clock, and other antiques.
When summer was over,
Mr. Frizzle put up a sign:

CLOSED UNTIL SPRING

One autumn, after he put up his sign,
Mr. Frizzle felt restless.
"I think I'll go
to sunny Mexico this winter," he said.
Off he went.
At first Gus liked living quietly
with Cora, Mouse, and Baby Ghost.
But winter was long
and the snow was so deep
that not even Mouse could go out.
Gus began to miss Frizzle
and Frizzle's shouting.

Then a picture postcard came,
showing beautiful Mexico.
Mr. Frizzle wrote, "Wish you were here."
Gus studied the pretty picture,
and he had an idea.
"Frizzle wishes we were there,"
he told Cora.
"We'll go to Mexico and surprise him!"

He found Mexico on a map.
He found the town where Mr. Frizzle was.
He put Baby Ghost in a blanket
and Cora in a basket.
"What about me?" snarled Mouse,
who was always unpleasant.
Gus told him that he could go
in the basket with Cora.
Mouse made a face, and said,
"Then I'll stay home."

Gus, Baby Ghost, and Cora
took an airplane to Mexico City.
They took a bus to the town
where Mr. Frizzle was staying.
When they arrived,
the sun was warm
and the sky was blue.
Flowers were in bloom.
"Very nice," said Gus.
"Now where's Frizzle?"

Cora said, "Meow!"
so he let her out of her basket.
They walked along little streets,
past pink and blue and white houses.
They saw women carrying babies in *rebozos*.
Gus bought a *rebozo*
for carrying Baby Ghost.
He also bought a sombrero.
They saw women selling *tortillas*,
and Gus bought one for Cora's lunch.

They saw women selling flowers,
men selling blankets,
artists painting pictures,

a little donkey
delivering water
in great big cans.

Cora saw lots of cats.
They didn't see Frizzle.

When it grew dark,
they saw fireworks.

Then they reached a park
filled with boys and girls.
The boys were parading
one way around the park,

so Gus, carrying Baby Ghost,
marched along too.
The girls paraded the other way,
and Cora joined them.

Gus kept looking for Frizzle.
"We must find a place to sleep," he said.
They walked down a street
and knocked on a door with a brass knocker.
A woman peeked out.
"Good evening, *señora*," said Gus.
"Would you have a room to rent to a ghost?"
"Certainly, Señor Yankee Ghost,"
the *señora* said.

She led them
through a patio
filled with flowers,
up a winding stair,
to a room with a balcony
and a fine view.

In the morning, Gus said,
"We'll find Frizzle today."
They walked up and down the streets.
They were passing two artists
seated at their easels, painting pictures,
when suddenly Gus stopped.
One of the artists was speaking.
"Cora!" gasped Gus. "That's Frizzle!"
Frizzle looked so healthy and happy
that he hardly knew him.
"Meow!" cried Cora joyfully,
and leaped on Frizzle's lap.
Mr. Frizzle couldn't see Gus,
as Gus was a ghost.
Not dreaming Cora
could be in Mexico
he thought she was
some strange Mexican cat
and pushed her off.

"As I was saying," he told his friend,
"Mexico is a fine place.
I like painting pictures too.
I think I'll stay here forever."
Gus was thunderstruck.
"He doesn't even know us!" he said.
"And he doesn't want to come home!"
What would happen
if Frizzle didn't go back?
A new man might not like ghosts and cats,
and Gus shuddered to think
what would befall Mouse.

"It's best he doesn't know
that we're here," he decided.
"I must put
some thoughts in his head at once."
So, in a ghostly way, he told Frizzle,
"You run a fine museum.
Don't you forget that!"
"Someone else can run my fine museum,"
Frizzle told his friend.
"You're very proud of that museum!"
Gus shouted in ghostly language.
"I'm proud of that museum," said Frizzle.
"But I'm tired of working.
I'm going to stay here in the sun
and paint pictures."
"I'll have to scare the fellow
out of Mexico," said Gus.

When the artists
folded their easels and went off,
Gus followed with Baby Ghost and Cora.
He found that Mr. Frizzle
had a room much like theirs.
Frizzle put his easel and paints
and the picture he was painting
in a corner and went out to dinner.
"Here I go," said Gus.
He dropped the picture on the floor.
Frizzle came back.
He picked up the picture.
"No harm done," he said.
He didn't know Gus had dropped the picture.

"I don't like to play tricks,
but what can I do?" said Gus.
He moved Mr. Frizzle's easel
across the room.
He threw his paints on the floor
and spilled the water.
He scattered brushes around.
"That girl who cleans my room
is mighty careless," Frizzle muttered.
He didn't know Gus had messed things up.

Still Mr. Frizzle was determined
to stay in Mexico.
"It's spring.
Time to open the Museum," said Gus.
"How can I get Frizzle back there?
I must take *drastic steps*."
So one night Mr. Frizzle's bed
began to shake.

Frizzle woke up and rushed out of the room.
"Are we having an earthquake?" he shouted.
"No, *señor*,"
said the people in the house with surprise.
"My bed was shaking,"
said Frizzle.
"Bad dream, *señor*,"
said the people.

When Mr. Frizzle
went out to paint
the next day,
he said to his friend,
"Strange things
are happening.
My easel moves around,
my pictures fall down,
and last night my bed shook."
Gus could see Frizzle was worried.
"We're getting somewhere now,"
he whispered to Cora.
Stranger things happened to Mr. Frizzle.
His easel broke.
His pictures danced around the room.
His brushes painted the wall.
The blankets were pulled off his bed.
But Frizzle wanted to stay in Mexico
and paint pictures!

"I wish I'd brought
my bang-clank equipment," said Gus.
"What can I get to make a big noise?
Aha! I know!"
He bought some fireworks.
"If these don't send him home,
nothing will!" Gus declared.
"You wait on Frizzle's balcony, Cora."
Then he stole into Frizzle's room
and set a match to the fireworks
in the middle of the floor.

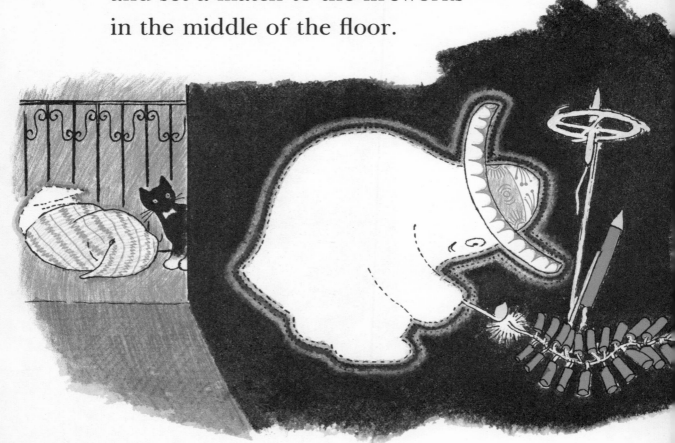

Whsst went the fireworks,
hitting the ceiling.
Bang, pop, pop. BANG!

Frizzle sprang from his bed.

The fireworks scared Cora and Baby Ghost.

"Meow, meow!" howled Cora.

"Wow, wow!" screamed Baby Ghost.

Frizzle almost died, he was so scared.

"I've got ghosts in my room!

Mexican ghosts!" he shouted.

"I'm going home!"

He was in such a hurry
that he didn't even take his easel.
"Good-by!" said Frizzle to the people,
and rushed to take a plane.
Gus hurried too.
He slapped his sombrero on his head.
He dumped Cora in her basket,
picked up Frizzle's easel and pictures,
and snatched up Baby Ghost.
They caught a plane before Mr. Frizzle's,
and they got home first.

"About time!" snapped Mouse,
coming to the door.
Gus tossed his sombrero on a table
and set up the easel,
which wasn't broken now,
with a picture
that Mr. Frizzle had painted.
He and Cora ran upstairs
to get settled.

Mr. Frizzle arrived.
The sky was blue, the breeze warm,
and flowers were coming up.
"I believe I'm glad to be home,"
said Mr. Frizzle.
He unlocked the door and went in.
Gus and Cora peeked down
from the top of the stairs,
holding their breath.
Mouse muttered.
Mr. Frizzle stared in bewilderment
at the easel he had left behind.
Then, on the table,
he saw a Mexican sombrero.
Slowly the truth dawned,
and Mr. Frizzle knew he had been tricked.
He could think of just one way
for the easel and sombrero to get there.
Gus!

"You confounded ghost!" roared Frizzle.
Then Gus and Cora
hugged each other and laughed
until they cried.
Frizzle was home.
Frizzle was shouting.
And all was well again.